Dear Parent:
Your child's love of reading starts here!

Every child learns to read in a different way and at his or her own speed. Some go back and forth between reading levels and read favorite books again and again. Others read through each level in order. You can help your young reader improve and become more confident by encouraging his or her own interests and abilities. From books your child reads with you to the first books he or she reads alone, there are I Can Read Books for every stage of reading:

SHARED READING
Basic language, word repetition, and whimsical illustrations, ideal for sharing with your emergent reader

BEGINNING READING
Short sentences, familiar words, and simple concepts for children eager to read on their own

READING WITH HELP
Engaging stories, longer sentences, and language play for developing readers

READING ALONE
Complex plots, challenging vocabulary, and high-interest topics for the independent reader

ADVANCED READING
Short paragraphs, chapters, and exciting themes for the perfect bridge to chapter books

I Can Read Books have introduced children to the joy of reading since 1957. Featuring award-winning authors and illustrators and a fabulous cast of beloved characters, I Can Read Books set the standard for beginning readers.

A lifetime of discovery begins with the magical words **"I Can Read!"**

Visit www.icanread.com for information
on enriching your child's reading experience.

Surprise! This is for Janet Ballou.
—J.O'C.

For my friends Audrey, Eloise, and Nicki Presby
—R.P.G.

For HM: Who threw me my once-and-only-ever,
kinda-sorta-mostly, actual real-life
"You got me!" surprise party
—T.E.

I Can Read Book® is an imprint of HarperCollins Publishers.

ISBN 978-0-06-226979-9 (trade bdg.)—ISBN 978-0-06-226978-2 (pbk.)

15 16 17 18 19   SCP   10 9 8 7 6 5 4 3 2 1   ❖   First Edition

Fancy NANCY

Super Secret Surprise Party

by Jane O'Connor

cover illustration by Robin Preiss Glasser

interior illustrations by Ted Enik

HARPER

An Imprint of HarperCollinsPublishers

Ooh la la!

Our class is throwing a party.

I can't reveal who it's for.

(Reveal is a fancy word for tell.)

I don't want to spoil the surprise.

"Everybody is on a committee.

A committee is a group

with a job to do,"

I tell my family at dinner.

"My committee is in charge
of refreshments."
Then I explain to my sister
that refreshments means food.

"Who is the party for?"

JoJo wants to know.

JoJo is not trustworthy.

She can't keep secrets.

So I say, "I am sorry.

I cannot tell you."

Then I lock my lips and throw

away the key.

The next day

our committee meets at recess.

Lionel will take care of beverages.

That's fancy for stuff to drink.

"I will bake cupcakes," I say.

Clara says,

"I'll bring chips

and popcorn for the party."

Uh-oh!

Grace overhears us.

That means she is listening in.

"Party? What party?"

she says really loudly.

Grace is not in our class.

She doesn't know about our party.

"*Shhhh.* It's a secret," I say.

"It's a surprise," says Lionel.

"You better invite me,"
Grace says.

Lionel shakes his head.

"Sorry. You can't come."

Right away

Grace starts yelling.

"That's mean!

I'm telling."

She points to Ms. Glass

and the other teachers.

Oh no!

She can't tell them.

It would be a disaster!

It would ruin everything.

We explain why the party is

just for our class.

"You have to keep it hush-hush,"
I say.

"You can't tell a soul."
Grace promises.

But Grace is not always trustworthy.
We make her lock her lips
and throw away the key.

After school,

Annie takes us shopping.

She is a teenager

and babysits for us sometimes.

Bree is on the decorating committee.
Decorating means making
our classroom look fancy.
She buys balloons and streamers.

We run into Robert.

He is on the supplies committee.

He is buying

paper plates and napkins.

"Who is the party for?" Annie asks.

Annie is very trustworthy.

So we confide in her.

(Confide is like reveal.

It's another fancy word for tell.)

Still we make Annie lock her lips

and throw away the key.

In the supermarket,

I buy a box of cupcake mix.

It is called Chocolate Surprise.

That is perfect

for a surprise party!

That night

Dad and I bake the cupcakes.

Then we frost them.

They are chocolate with

tiny marshmallows inside.

The marshmallows are the surprise.

The next morning

everyone in our class

comes to school very early.

We decorate the room.

Yoko has made a giant card.

All it needs is our signatures.

Signature is fancy for writing out

your name.

So? Have you guessed

who the surprise party is for?

Yes! It's for Ms. Glass!

She walks in

and we all shout, "Surprise!

Happy birthday!"

Ms. Glass is so surprised,
she can't say a word.
She is speechless.

We give Ms. Glass the card.

We sing "Happy Birthday."

Then we have juice and cupcakes.

Mmmmm. The cupcakes are delectable.

That's fancy for yummy.

"So how old are you, Ms. Glass?"

Lionel wants to know.

Ms. Glass smiles.

"That's a secret," she says.

Then she locks her lips

and throws away the key.

Fancy Nancy's Fancy Words

These are the fancy words in this book:

Beverages—drinks

Committee—a group with a job to do

Confide—tell

Decorating—making something look fancy

Delectable—yummy

Overhears—listens in

Refreshments—food

Reveal—that means tell, too

Signature—writing out your name

Trustworthy—able to keep secrets